Chapter 1: Timmy's Curiosi

Timmy, a bright-eyed and adventurous young boy, was spending his summer break at his grandma's house. Every day, he would explore every nook and cranny, searching for hidden treasures and fascinating secrets. On one particularly hot and sunny afternoon, Timmy decided to venture into the musty attic.

As he climbed the wooden stairs, the air grew heavy, filled with the scent of dust and old memories. The attic was a treasure trove of forgotten heirlooms, each covered with a thin layer of age. Timmy's eyes lit up with excitement as he surveyed the room, filled with antique furniture, old trunks, and stacks of yellowed books.

His curious nature drew him closer to an intriguing antique chest tucked away in a dim corner. The chest was beautifully crafted with intricate carvings depicting scenes from a distant era. Dust danced around as Timmy traced the patterns with his fingers, his mind brimming with wonder.

Unable to contain his eagerness, Timmy slowly lifted the heavy lid of the chest. A cloud of dust engulfed the attic, and Timmy coughed as he peered inside. Hidden beneath layers of old fabric, he discovered a seemingly ordinary wooden box. But this box held a secret. It wasn't just any box; it was home to Boxley, a mischievous sprite.

As Timmy's eyes adjusted to the dim light, he noticed a flurry of movement from within the box. Curiosity stirred inside him, urging him to investigate further. He carefully opened the box, and to his astonishment, there stood a petite creature with delicate, translucent wings—Boxley, the sprite.

Boxley blinked his emerald green eyes, momentarily startled by the sudden brightness. But soon, a playful grin spread across his tiny face as he saw Timmy standing there, spellbound by a world beyond his imagination.

"Hello there, young explorer," Boxley chimed, his voice tinkling like wind chimes on a summer breeze.

Timmy's eyes widened with a mixture of surprise and delight. Never had he imagined that a wondrous creature like Boxley could exist. "Who... who are you?" he stammered, struggling to contain his excitement.

"I am Boxley, a sprite from a realm unseen," he replied, floating effortlessly in front of Timmy. "And it seems that your curiosity has awakened my slumber."

Timmy's heart raced with anticipation as he realized the incredible adventure unfolding before him. "How can I see this hidden realm? Can you teach me how to travel to where you're from?" he asked, his voice filled with hope.

With a mischievous twinkle in his eyes, Boxley nodded. "Oh, Timmy, dear friend, just follow my lead. With your open mind and eager heart, together, we shall explore realms both near and far."

In that moment, Timmy and Boxley formed an unbreakable bond, destined to embark on countless extraordinary journeys. The attic, once filled with forgotten treasures, was now a gateway to whole new worlds waiting to be discovered.

As the sun began to set, casting a warm golden glow over the attic, Timmy and Boxley huddled together, hearts brimming with excitement, plotting their next grand adventure. Little did they know, the antique chest was merely the beginning of the incredible tales that awaited them.

And so, with curiosity as their guiding light, Timmy and Boxley prepared to set off on extraordinary adventures, where countless wonders and magical beings would soon cross their path. Chapter 1 marked the awakening of Timmy's curiosity, unveiling a world far beyond his wildest dreams.

Chapter 2: Boxley's Playful Mischief

Timmy woke up the next morning, eager to see what adventure awaited him and Boxley. As he entered the living room, he noticed that the room seemed different somehow. The furniture was rearranged, and there were toys scattered all over the floor.

"Boxley, what have you been up to?" Timmy asked, marveling at the chaotic scene.

With a mischievous grin, Boxley appeared from behind the couch. "I thought our living room needed a little excitement, so I decided to give it a makeover," he chirped.

Timmy couldn't help but laugh. Boxley had transformed their once orderly living room into a playful wonderland. The coffee table was now a fort made from cushions and blankets, and the floor was covered in a colorful array of toys.

"Come on, Timmy! Let's embark on a grand adventure in our new fort. We can be pirates sailing through treacherous waters," Boxley suggested, his eyes sparkling with excitement.

Timmy couldn't resist Boxley's infectious enthusiasm. "Arr, matey! Lead the way, Captain Boxley!" Timmy exclaimed.

For hours, the two friends sailed their imaginary ship, battling imaginary sea monsters and finding hidden treasures. They laughed and shouted with joy, their spirits lifted by Boxley's mischievous creativity.

As the day wore on, Timmy realized that Boxley's penchant for mischief extended beyond their playroom. During their afternoon walk in the park, Boxley couldn't resist pulling pranks on unsuspecting passersby. He tickled dogs' noses, causing them to chase their tails, and tied colorful ribbons on people's backpacks, creating a trail of confusion.

"Boxley, you're such a trickster!" Timmy giggled, trying to catch his breath after another one of Boxley's playful escapades.

"But isn't it fun, Timmy? The world needs a little mischief now and then. It makes people smile and brings joy to their lives," Boxley explained, his eyes twinkling with mischief.

Timmy couldn't argue with that. He had seen how people's faces lit up with laughter and surprise whenever Boxley was around. His friend's playful spirit brought a sense of adventure and delight to their otherwise ordinary days.

As the sun began to set, signaling the end of their playtime, Timmy and Boxley returned home, leaving a trail of giggling children and curious adults behind them. They were tired but exhilarated, grateful for the joy that Boxley had brought into their lives.

That night, as they settled down for bed, Timmy thanked Boxley for the exciting day they had shared. Boxley snuggled up next to him and whispered, "Timmy, life is an adventure waiting to unfold. With a dash of mischief, we can make even the quietest moments memorable."

Timmy smiled, realizing that his life had become richer and more vibrant since Boxley had entered it. As he drifted off to sleep, a mischievous sparkle danced in his dreams, promising more exciting adventures with his playful sprite friend, Boxley.

Chapter 3: A Walk in the Enchanted Forest

As the sun began to set on a bright and sunny day, Timmy and his loyal friend Boxley the sprite decided it was the perfect time to explore the enchanted forest. Excitement sparkled in their eyes as they stood at the edge of the forest, gazing at the towering trees and mysterious glimmering lights deep within.

Timmy took a deep breath, inhaling the sweet scent of flowers and adventure that filled the air. He took a step forward, feeling the soft forest floor beneath his feet. Boxley grinned mischievously, his tiny wings buzzing with anticipation.

The moment they stepped foot into the enchanted forest, it was as if they had entered a whole new world. The trees stood tall and proud, their branches intertwining and forming a magical canopy above, casting delightful shadows on the ground below. The rustling leaves whispered secrets as if inviting the duo to explore further.

Every step they took revealed new wonders. Delicate flowers painted in vibrant hues lined their path, their petals shimmering with a radiant glow. Timmy knelt down to touch one, and as his fingers brushed against the silky petals, the flower giggled and fluttered its dainty wings in delight.

Boxley flew ahead, his tiny wings carrying him effortlessly through the enchanting forest. He danced from branch to branch, his mischievous spirit infecting even the most stoic of creatures. Squirrels chased each other playfully, butterflies intertwined in a whimsical ballet, and songbirds filled the air with sweet melodies.

Curiosity sparked within Timmy's heart as he ventured deeper into the forest. The sunlight peeked through the dense foliage, casting ethereal rays that illuminated the magical creatures they encountered. Timmy's eyes widened in awe as he saw an enchanting unicorn grazing on a carpet of glittering moss, its mane glistening like a river of stardust.

Further along their path, a mischievous group of fairies danced and circled in the air, their tiny wings creating a mesmerizing display of colors. Timmy and Boxley watched, their hearts filled with wonder, as the fairies left trails of sparkling dust in their wake. It was as if pixie dust had been scattered all around, turning the forest into a place of enchantment.

As the day turned into dusk, the duo stumbled upon a hidden clearing. The ground beneath their feet was covered in a luminescent carpet of mushrooms, each glowing in a different hue. Timmy and Boxley sat down amidst the glow, letting the serene beauty of the forest wash over them.

In that moment, they realized that the enchanted forest was not just a place of adventure but a haven of peace, magic, and unimaginable wonder. With joy and contentment radiating from their hearts, Timmy and Boxley made a pact to return to this enchanted haven, to explore and discover the secrets of the forest together.

As the stars began to twinkle overhead, Timmy and Boxley bid farewell to the enchanted forest, knowing that their journey had only just begun. With memories of magical creatures, shimmering plants, and whimsical landscapes filling their minds, the duo headed back home, eagerly looking forward to their next adventure.

Little did they know, the enchanted forest held countless mysteries and marvels just waiting to be unveiled, and Timmy and Boxley were ready to unlock its secrets with each step they took.

Chapter 4: Timmy Meets the Wise Owl

As Timmy and Boxley ventured deeper into the enchanted forest, a sense of wonder filled the air. The trees seemed to whisper secrets to one another, and the light that filtered through the leaves created a magical ambiance. Timmy could barely contain his excitement as he wondered what other enchanting creatures he would encounter in this mystical place.

Suddenly, a hoot resonated through the forest, and Timmy looked up to see a magnificent owl perched on a branch above them. Its piercing eyes seemed to look straight into Timmy's soul, as if they held the answers to all the mysteries of the forest.

"Hello there, young travelers," the wise old owl spoke in a voice tinged with wisdom. "What brings you to my domain?"

Timmy, slightly dazed by the owl's awe-inspiring presence, introduced himself and Boxley. "We've always been curious about the enchanted forest," Timmy explained, "and we want to learn all we can about its secrets."

The owl's eyes twinkled, and a wry smile formed on its beak. "Ah, curiosity is a wonderful trait, young one. The enchanted forest is a place of ancient wonders and deep mysteries. Have you heard about the Whispering Grove?"

Timmy and Boxley exchanged glances, both shaking their heads. "No, we haven't," Timmy replied eagerly. "What is the Whispering Grove? Is it a magical place?"

The owl nodded solemnly. "Indeed, it is. Legend has it that within the grove, trees communicate in a language only they understand. They share stories of long-forgotten kingdoms, mythical creatures, and even future events. But gaining entry to the Whispering Grove is no easy feat. It requires a brave heart and a sincere desire to protect the forest."

Timmy was captivated by the owl's words. He had always dreamed of exploring hidden realms and unraveling mysteries. "I promise I will return, oh wise owl," Timmy declared, determination shining in his eyes. "With Boxley by my side, we will unlock the secrets of the Whispering Grove."

The owl chuckled softly, its feathers ruffling. "I sense determination in your voice, young Timmy. If your intentions are pure, the forest will guide you. But remember, the enchanted forest is a delicate ecosystem that must be respected. Take only memories and leave no trace."

Timmy nodded, understanding the owl's warning. He knew that the forest was not merely a playground for his adventures but a living organism deserving of his utmost care and respect.

With newfound knowledge in his heart and a promise on his lips, Timmy bid farewell to the wise old owl. As he and Boxley made their way back through the forest, their steps were lighter, filled with anticipation for the journey that awaited them. They couldn't wait to return to the Whispering Grove and uncover the secrets hidden within.

Little did they know that this encounter was only the beginning of their extraordinary adventures in the enchanted forest, where every step brought them closer to unraveling the forest's ancient secrets.

Chapter 5: Magical Lessons with Boxley

Timmy was thrilled when Boxley, his tiny sprite friend, offered to teach him the wonders of magic. He couldn't wait to embark on this new adventure with his loyal companion. With twinkling eyes and a mischievous grin, Boxley led Timmy deep into the Enchanted Forest, where an ancient, grand oak tree stood tall.

Under the shade of the oak tree, Boxley conjured a small, wooden table and two comfortable chairs. He gestured for Timmy to sit down, and as he did, a pile of spellbooks appeared before him.

"Alright, Timmy," Boxley said, fluttering his wings. "Today, we shall start with the basics of spellcasting."

Eagerly, Timmy opened the first spellbook, revealing a page filled with intricate symbols and incantations. Boxley began explaining the importance of proper pronunciation and concentration while casting spells. Timmy listened attentively, absorbing every word.

"Now, let's try a simple levitation spell," Boxley suggested, pointing to a levitation charm in one of the spellbooks. "Repeat after me, Timmy. Zephyr levito!"

Timmy imitated Boxley, his voice wavering at first but growing more confident with each repetition. Suddenly, a tiny gust of wind emerged, lifting a pebble off the ground. Timmy's eyes widened with amazement.

"Well done, Timmy!" Boxley exclaimed, clapping his hands. "You've successfully cast your first spell!"

From that day forward, Timmy and Boxley spent countless hours practicing and mastering spells together. They learned how to create illusions, summon small creatures, and even manipulate fire and water. Timmy's skills improved with each passing day, and he marveled at the magical possibilities that lay before him.

As their bond grew stronger, Boxley shared tales of his Sprite ancestry and the enchanted realms he had visited throughout his long life. Timmy absorbed every bit of knowledge, his imagination running wild with excitement.

One day, Boxley introduced Timmy to the art of potion brewing. They gathered rare herbs and ingredients from the Enchanted Forest and began crafting their first potion. As they mixed, stirred, and chanted ancient incantations, a vibrant, sparkling vial of liquid grew before them.

"Behold, Timmy! This is the Potion of Invisibility," Boxley exclaimed, holding up the vial. "With this potion, you can become unseen to the naked eye."

Curiosity twinkled in Timmy's eyes as Boxley handed him the vial. He cautiously took a sip, and in an instant, he disappeared.

Timmy and Boxley burst into laughter, reveling in the newfound magic. With his invisible form, Timmy pranked his friends and family, their bewildered expressions bringing joy to his heart.

From that day on, Timmy and Boxley were an inseparable duo, their enchanting escapades taking them to extraordinary places. Together, they explored hidden caves and ancient ruins, encountering mythical creatures and overcoming thrilling challenges using their combined magical abilities.

With Boxley by his side, Timmy's world had transformed into a realm of endless possibilities. And as their knowledge of magic deepened, their bond grew stronger, prepared to face any adventure that awaited them.

The adventures of Timmy and Boxley were only beginning. Many more mesmerizing lessons and captivating escapades awaited them in their extraordinary journey through the enchanted realms of magic.

Chapter 6: A Rescue Mission Begins

Excitement filled the air as Timmy and Boxley received urgent news from the enchanted forest. A baby dragon had been captured by an evil sorceress named Malena. The poor creature was held captive in a dark and gloomy castle atop the highest mountain.

Timmy and Boxley shared a deep concern for any helpless creature in need. Their hearts echoed with a common desire to rescue the baby dragon and free it from Malena's clutches. With determination blazing in their eyes, they wasted no time in devising a plan.

As seasoned adventurers, Timmy and Boxley knew they needed a strategy to outwit the evil sorceress. Boxley, being a sprite with magical abilities, revealed his plan to Timmy. "We'll need to be swift and clever," Boxley said. "I can disguise myself as a mischievous imp and act as a distraction while you sneak into the castle."

Timmy nodded, impressed by Boxley's cunning plan. He fetched his trusty map from his backpack, unfurled it, and studied it intently. Together, they plotted their path, avoiding treacherous terrain, and marking potential obstacles along the way.

The journey to the castle was arduous, but Timmy and Boxley remained undeterred. They trekked through tangled vines, crossed raging rivers, and climbed steep cliffs, their determination fueling their every step.

Finally, after days of relentless pursuit, they reached the formidable castle. Its towering spires pierced the sky, casting long shadows over the surrounding landscape. Gargoyles perched menacingly on the battlements, their eyes seemingly following their every move.

With hearts pounding, Timmy and Boxley put their plan into action. Boxley transformed into a mischievous imp, cackling with a wicked twinkle in his eye. He danced and pranced in front of the castle gates, creating a ruckus that caught the attention of Malena's guards.

While the guards were distracted by Boxley's antics, Timmy slipped past them unnoticed. He moved with silent precision, blending into the shadows as he made his way deeper into the castle. Each step carried him closer to his ultimate goal: rescuing the baby dragon.

Chapter 7: The Sorceress's Lair

Timmy and Boxley cautiously approached the entrance of the sorceress's lair. The ancient stone door towered above them, covered in mystical carvings that seemed to come alive as they got closer. Timmy could feel his heart pounding with excitement, mixed with a tinge of fear.

"Are you sure about this, Boxley?" Timmy whispered, looking at the mischievous sprite perched on his shoulder.

Boxley, with his twinkling eyes and mischievous grin, gave Timmy a confident nod. "Of course, Timmy! We've come so far, and we can't turn back now. We have to stop the sorceress from using her powers for evil."

With determination fueling their every step, Timmy and Boxley pushed open the massive door, revealing a dark and eerie chamber. Strange symbols glowed on the floor, creating an intimidating path deeper into the lair.

As they ventured forward, their footsteps echoed through the labyrinthine hallways. Suddenly, a thick fog engulfed them, making it almost impossible to see. Timmy stumbled, almost losing his balance, but Boxley swiftly caught him.

"I can't see a thing, Boxley!" Timmy exclaimed, his voice trembling slightly.

"Don't worry, Timmy," Boxley reassured him. "I've got an idea!"

With a snap of his tiny fingers, Boxley summoned a glowing orb of light, dispelling the fog that had surrounded them. Timmy's eyes widened in awe as the colorful light bathed the area, revealing hidden paths and narrow walkways.

As they continued on, they encountered a series of magically animated statues, each guarding a separate corridor. The stone warriors lunged at them with swords swinging, but Timmy and Boxley swiftly dodged every attack with acrobatic moves and quick thinking.

Reaching the final challenge, they stood before a massive door guarded by enormous fire-breathing sentinels. Realizing that courage and quick reflexes alone wouldn't help them this time, Boxley flew into action.

He began to sing a spell, his ethereal voice filling the air.

As Boxley sang, the sentinels' flames turned a calming blue, transforming their fiery dispositions into peaceful protectors. With the danger diminished, Timmy and Boxley opened the grand door, revealing the inner sanctum of the sorceress.

Entering cautiously, they found the sorceress standing in front of an emerald-encrusted pedestal. She turned to face them, her eyes full of anger at their intrusion.

"You dare to challenge me?" she hissed, her voice dripping with malice.

Timmy, with a newfound confidence, stepped forward. "You may have power, sorceress, but we have something stronger. We have friendship and love."

Boxley nodded in agreement. "That's right! You may have all the magic in the world, but you won't triumph over the bond we share."

The sorceress sneered, but as she attempted to cast a spell, her powers flickered and faltered. The strength of Timmy and Boxley's friendship disrupted her dark magic.

With their combined wit and courage, Timmy and Boxley managed to outsmart the sorceress and undo her evil enchantments. The magical energy returned to its rightful balance, and the lair began to crumble around them.

As it all fell apart, Timmy and Boxley raced to the exit, their hearts pounding with adrenaline. They had successfully defeated the sorceress and reclaimed peace for their world.

Emerging into the sunlight, Timmy and Boxley shared a heartfelt moment, knowing their journey wasn't just about stopping evil. It was about the unbreakable bond they had formed and the incredible adventures they would continue to face together.

And so, as Timmy and Boxley walked away, triumph evident in their steps, they prepared themselves for the next great adventure that awaited them beyond the sorceress's lair.

Chapter 8: Saving the Dragon

Timmy and Boxley cautiously entered the dimly lit lair, their hearts pounding with both fear and determination. The walls were lined with ancient runes and glowing crystals, giving off an ethereal glow. As they moved deeper into the lair, they could hear the faint sound of whimpering coming from behind a sturdy iron door.

They reached the source of the sound and discovered a baby dragon, its majestic wings bound with thick chains and its vibrant scales dulled by despair. It looked up at Timmy and Boxley with wide, fearful eyes. Timmy's heart ached at the sight of such a magnificent creature imprisoned and tortured.

"We have to save it, Boxley," Timmy whispered, fear mingled with determination in his voice.

Boxley nodded, his sprite wings shimmering in agreement. "We'll need to use our magical abilities to break these chains and set the dragon free," he suggested.

Together, Timmy and Boxley closed their eyes, focusing their minds and tapping into the magical energy that flowed within them. They channeled their powers toward the chains, summoning a burst of blue light that engulfed the bindings.

With a resounding crack, the chains shattered and fell to the ground. The dragon, now free from its restraints, let out a mighty roar of relief, causing the lair to tremble. It nuzzled against Timmy and Boxley, its gratitude evident in its eyes.

As they gazed into the dragon's eyes, a connection formed between them. Timmy felt a rush of warmth and strength, as if the dragon was sharing its own ancient power with him. Boxley, too, felt the bond growing stronger, a unity between sprite and dragon.

With newfound confidence, Timmy and Boxley led the dragon out of the lair, guiding it to a secret path that would take them to safety.

As they emerged into the sunlight, villagers who had been living in fear of the dragon's wrath gasped in astonishment. But instead of seeing a fearsome creature, they saw a majestic dragon, now free and filled with gratitude.

Timmy addressed the villagers, his voice strong and filled with authority. "This dragon is not a threat to anyone. It was imprisoned and tortured, its true nature suppressed. We have set it free, and now it will be a protector of our land, never to cause harm again."

The villagers, initially skeptical, began to see the truth in Timmy's words. They marveled at the sight of the dragon's power and grace. Slowly, their fear turned to awe and respect.

From that day forward, Timmy, Boxley, and the dragon formed an unbreakable bond. The dragon, now known as Ember, became a guardian of the land, protecting it from those who sought to harm it. Timmy and Boxley were celebrated as heroes, their bravery and magical abilities admired by all.

In the end, Timmy and Boxley had not only saved a dragon but had restored hope and unity to their land. They proved that sometimes, even the most misunderstood creatures can become the greatest allies, and that true power lies in empathy and compassion.

Chapter 9: A Friendship Strained

Timmy and Boxley had always been as thick as thieves, their friendship forged through countless adventures. But one sunny afternoon, it seemed that the bonds of their friendship would be put to the ultimate test.

Timmy's family had invited their relatives over for a grand barbecue in their backyard. It was an important occasion as they hadn't seen each other in years. With laughter and excitement filling the air, everyone eagerly awaited the feast.

Timmy, being the thoughtful young boy he was, tried to help his mother with the preparations. He stacked chairs, set the table, and even helped his father set up the grill. Boxley, always brimming with mischief, couldn't resist the temptation to join in on all the fun.

As the guests began arriving, Boxley decided to entertain them with his magical spritely tricks. He fluttered around, leaving trails of shimmering pixie dust and pulling small pranks on unsuspecting family members. At first, the trickery charmed everyone, eliciting laughter and surprise.

However, Boxley's mischievous nature got the better of him, and he accidentally tripped Timmy's cousin, Sarah, causing her to drop her precious jewelry box. The box shattered into a thousand pieces, leaving Sarah heartbroken.

Timmy's family was still trying to console Sarah when Boxley, realizing the gravity of his actions, became consumed with guilt. He had never wanted to harm anyone, let alone hurt Timmy's family.

Timmy's face flushed with anger and disappointment. His eyes brimmed with unshed tears as he stared at Boxley. "How could you do this? I trusted you!" Timmy's voice quivered with hurt.

Boxley, regret etched on his face, flew over to Timmy's side. "I'm so sorry, Timmy. I never meant for this to happen. It was just a harmless trick gone wrong."

Tears streamed down Timmy's face as he struggled to contain his emotions. "I trusted you, Boxley. To be my friend and not cause trouble for my family. I don't know if I can forgive you."

The atmosphere became heavy with tension, and the beautiful day felt overshadowed by their disagreement. Boxley felt his heart sink, realizing how much he had hurt the friend he cherished most.

In that moment, both Timmy and Boxley knew that their friendship hung in the balance. Timmy's anger and disappointment were valid, but deep down, he understood that Boxley never meant any harm.

Taking a deep breath, Boxley mustered the courage to speak. "Timmy, I know I can't undo what happened. But please believe me when I say that your friendship means the world to me. I promise to make it right, somehow."

Timmy looked into Boxley's sincere eyes, seeing the remorse and love that remained. He realized that his friendship with Boxley was built on countless adventures, shared laughter, and an unbreakable bond. Slowly releasing his anger, Timmy nodded, forgiving Boxley.

As the day went on, Timmy and Boxley worked together to make amends for

Boxley's mischief. With their combined ingenuity, they managed to repair Sarah's jewelry box and surprise her with a handmade necklace to replace the broken one.

Through their collective efforts, Timmy's family forgave Boxley, understanding that it was an innocent mistake. The laughter and joy returned to the party, and the day ended on a high note.

Timmy and Boxley emerged from this challenging experience with a deeper appreciation for one another. Their friendship had grown stronger, for they had realized that forgiveness, understanding, and love were the foundations upon which true friendship was built.

As they watched the sun set, casting a warm glow on their renewed bond, Timmy and Boxley knew that no matter the hurdles they faced, their friendship would always prevail. And together, they eagerly awaited their next adventure, knowing that they were ready to conquer any challenge that came their way.

Chapter 10: Searching for Lost Fairy Tales

Timmy and Boxley had spent weeks exploring the enchanted forest, but their latest discovery was truly extraordinary. As they ventured deeper into the dense woods, Timmy stumbled upon an old, dusty manuscript hidden beneath a moss-covered rock.

Excitedly, Timmy called out to Boxley, who emerged from a nearby tree as a mischievous sprite, always ready for a new adventure. Together, they carefully brushed off the dirt and opened the manuscript, revealing pages filled with faded ink and beautiful illustrations.

"This must be a book of lost fairy tales!" Timmy exclaimed, his eyes widening with excitement. "Look, Boxley! These are stories that haven't been told in ages!"

Boxley, already scanning the pages, nodded eagerly. "Indeed, Timmy! And it seems like these tales have lost their inhabitants too," he replied, his tiny wings fluttering with anticipation. "We must find them and bring these forgotten stories back to life!"

With newfound purpose, Timmy and Boxley began their quest. The first story they encountered was "The Tale of the Dancing Princesses," a beloved legend that had vanished from memory. Following the instructions in the manuscript, they embarked on a journey to a forgotten realm called Twilight Valley, where the princesses had disappeared.

As they entered the mystical valley, the surroundings grew dimmer, and a peculiar silence filled the air. The duo's senses heightened as they explored the concealed passages and secret tunnels, following the ghostly echo of tinkling laughter. Suddenly, they stumbled upon a hidden chamber glowing with dancing shoes and dresses.

Inside this enchanting room, Timmy and Boxley found the dancing princesses, their once sparkling spirits now subdued. With compassionate hearts, they revealed themselves as the bearers of the lost tale, promising to return the princesses' story to the world. As Timmy read the words aloud, the princesses' magic reignited, and their dance filled Twilight Valley with joy once more.

Moved by the success of their first mission, Timmy and Boxley's determination grew stronger. They flipped through the manuscript, discovering tales of talking animals, magical mirrors, and invisible cloaks. Each story led them to a new corner of the enchanted forest, where dormant characters awaited their revival.

Throughout their expedition, Timmy and Boxley encountered a timid rabbit named Harper, trapped in a fear-induced labyrinth, and brought her back to the vibrant world of "The Bunny and the Magic Meadow." They met a stubborn gnome named Grumble, locked away inside a decaying tree, and liberated him into the captivating tale of "The Lost Key to the Gnome Kingdom."

As the heroes followed the manuscript's guidance, Timmy and Boxley's bond deepened. Together, they realized the significance of their quest—to restore a world where fairy tales flourished, where magic and imagination intertwined.

With each tale, the enchantment of the forest grew stronger, its colors vivid, and its inhabitants filled with hope. As word of their adventures spread, other magical beings began to reappear, drawn by the joy and promise of the revitalized tales.

And so, Timmy and Boxley ventured forth, their hearts filled with determination, ready to find the forgotten characters and return the lost fairy tales to the world. They knew that every tale they brought to life would create a ripple of magic, ensuring the enduring power of imagination and the limitless possibilities that inhabited the hearts of young and old alike.

Together, Timmy and Boxley would be the guardians of these lost stories, preserving their enchantment for generations to come. And as they continued their quest, their bond of friendship grew, and their spirits soared, ready for whatever dangers and delights awaited them on the next page of this incredible adventure.

Chapter 11: A Visit to Mermaid Cove

Timmy and Boxley's curiosity had taken them to many astonishing places, but nothing compared to the underwater world they were about to discover. Armed with their newfound knowledge about the importance of preserving the environment, the pair embarked on their most intriguing adventure yet – a journey to the depths of the ocean.

Timmy, wearing a specially crafted breathing suit, and Boxley, floating alongside him, ventured into the vast ocean. As they swam deeper, the water around them turned a mesmerizing shade of blue, and the sunlight became a dim, shimmering glow.

It wasn't long before the pair stumbled upon an enormous gate. Decorated with beautiful seashells and coral, it signaled the entrance to Mermaid Cove — a magical underwater kingdom ruled by mermaids.

The gatekeeper, a friendly seahorse named Finn, welcomed Timmy and Boxley with a warm smile. He led them through a vibrant coral reef, where colorful fish danced in unison and rays of sunlight created breathtaking patterns on the ocean floor.

As they ventured deeper into Mermaid Cove, the sound of enchanting melodies filled the water. Timmy and Boxley followed the harmonious tunes until they arrived at a grand palace fashioned entirely out of seashells and pearls.

Inside, they were greeted by Queen Marina, a wise and graceful mermaid with a golden crown atop her flowing blue hair. Her eyes sparkled with wisdom and kindness as she welcomed the visitors.

Curiosity brimming, Timmy told Queen Marina about their recent adventures and what they had learned about protecting the environment. The queen nodded approvingly, impressed by their knowledge and passion.

Queen Marina took Timmy and Boxley on a tour of Mermaid Cove, showcasing its diverse marine life and the magical wonders hiding beneath the surface. They marveled at schools of rainbow-colored fish darting through the coral reefs and gasped in awe as they swam alongside graceful dolphins performing acrobatics.

Yet, as the tour continued, Timmy couldn't help but notice something troubling. He saw plastic bags and discarded waste polluting the clear blue waters, and the coral reefs starting to lose their vibrant colors.

Disturbed by what he saw, Timmy asked Queen Marina about the pollution. The queen sighed, explaining that human actions sometimes led to unintended consequences for the ocean. She stressed the importance of taking responsibility for preserving the beauty of the underwater world.

Timmy and Boxley felt a pang of guilt, realizing their own impact on the environment. They vowed to spread the message of conservation, starting with their own community.

Queen Marina smiled at their determination. She gifted them with enchanted seashells that allowed them to communicate with sea creatures, urging them to seek help whenever needed.

As Timmy and Boxley bid farewell to Mermaid Cove, their hearts were filled with a newfound sense of purpose. They promised to protect their oceans and spread awareness about preserving the environment.

Swimming back to the surface, they now felt a deeper connection to the world beneath the waves. Their adventure had awakened a passion within them, and they were determined to make a difference – not only for themselves but for all the creatures that called the ocean home.

And so, Timmy and Boxley surfaced with a renewed purpose, ready to embark on their next adventure – spreading the word about the beauty of the underwater world and the importance of preserving it for generations to come.

Chapter 12: A Dance in the Sky

Timmy had always dreamed of flying. He would often spend hours gazing up at the sky, wishing that he could soar high above the world below. Little did he know, his dream was about to come true.

One sunny afternoon, Timmy and Boxley found themselves standing at the edge of a clearing in the magical forest. The air was filled with excitement as the playful breeze whispered tales of grand adventures. Boxley, with mischievous eyes glistening, turned to Timmy and said, "Close your eyes, my friend. It's time for us to dance in the sky."

Curiosity tingled within Timmy as he obediently closed his eyes. Suddenly, he felt a soft, warm breeze and the sensation of weightlessness.

"Open your eyes, Timmy!" Boxley exclaimed.

Timmy gasped in awe as he found himself floating in the air. His heart fluttered at the sight of fluffy white clouds beneath his feet. The sky, once a distant dream, was now his playground.

With Boxley by his side, Timmy twirled and pirouetted through the sky, their laughter echoing through the heavens. They weaved in and out of the cotton candy-like clouds, their fingers grazing the softness as they glided effortlessly.

As they flew higher, they discovered a hidden world beyond the clouds. Colorful rainbows stretched across the sky, and tiny sprites danced on the rainbow's arches, painting the world with vibrant hues.

Boxley and Timmy joined the sprites, their feet barely touching the rainbows. Together, they danced to the melody of the wind, their every movement painting the sky with love and joy. Timmy's heart swelled with happiness as he twirled and leaped, his dream fulfilled in the most magical way imaginable.

They bobbed and weaved through the clouds, playing tag with the sun's rays that kissed their cheeks. Timmy's imagination bloomed like a thousand wildflowers, taking him to places he had never dreamt of before. They met friendly sky creatures, like the jovial cloud elephants and the graceful sky dolphins, who accompanied them on their journey.

After hours of enchanting flight, as the golden sun began to set, Timmy and Boxley reluctantly descended from the sky. They landed softly back in the clearing where it all began, but their hearts were still soaring high above the treetops.

As the day drew to a close, Timmy and Boxley sat side by side, their faces glowing with the memories of their sky dance. They held hands, knowing that their bond had grown even stronger during their exhilarating adventure.

With a sense of contentment, Timmy whispered to Boxley, "Thank you for showing me that dreams really do come true, especially when you have a true friend like you."

Boxley smiled warmly, his eyes gleaming with silent gratitude. Little did they know that this dance in the sky was just the beginning of the grander adventures awaiting them in the magical forest.

And so, with hearts full of wonder, Timmy and Boxley bid farewell to the sky and stepped into the forest, ready to embark on their next extraordinary journey.

Chapter 13: The Secret of the Whispering Winds

Timmy and Boxley had always been drawn to the heart of the forest. Its green canopy, towering trees, and unknown wonders pulled them deeper into its embrace. On this particular day, their journey led them to a hidden glen, where whispers seemed to dance through the air.

Curiosity filled their hearts as they followed the soft whispers that seemed to be calling them deeper into the forest. The sunlight filtered through the leaves, painting a mottled pattern on the ground. Timmy's eyes widened as he saw a radiant glow up ahead, emanating from a swirling vortex of sparkling golden dust. Boxley, the iridescent sprite, fluttered eagerly by Timmy's side.

"Timmy, do you hear those whispers too?" Boxley asked, her voice a gentle melody.

"Yes, Boxley," Timmy whispered back, his eyes never leaving the mysterious vortex. "It's like the forest is trying to tell us something."

Hand in hand, they cautiously stepped forward, transfixed by the magical scene unfolding before them. Within the vortex, they saw glimpses of different places and what seemed like moments frozen in time. They watched in awe as animals frolicked in meadows, knights battled mighty dragons, and fantastical creatures sang and danced.

As they approached, the whispers grew louder, and the duo felt a wave of energy envelop them. It felt familiar, as though the secret of their own abilities had been saved for this moment. The air around them crackled with magic, swirling and twirling like the leaves in a storm.

Suddenly, a figure materialized from the golden dust. She was a radiant woman with long flowing hair and eyes filled with ancient wisdom. Her ethereal countenance exuded power beyond imagination. Boxley recognized her right away as a guardian of the Whispering Winds.

"Welcome, Timmy and Boxley," the figure spoke, her voice carried by the whispers of the wind. "You have both been chosen to unlock the secrets of this magical realm, for within you lies extraordinary potential."

Timmy and Boxley exchanged wide-eyed glances, their hearts pounding with a mixture of fear and excitement.

"Tell us," Timmy said, his voice quivering with anticipation. "What are we capable of?"

The guardian's eyes sparkled with delight as she extended her hand towards them. "You possess the ability to bring harmony where there is chaos, to heal where there is pain, and to restore balance where there is imbalance. The Whispering Winds have chosen you to protect and nurture the magic of this forest."

Silently, Boxley and Timmy took the guardian's hand, feeling an immense surge of power and energy flow through them. In that moment, they knew they were destined for greatness.

With their newfound knowledge and purpose, Timmy and Boxley stood tall, ready to embrace their roles as guardians of the Whispering Winds. They vowed to protect the magic of the forest and ensure its balance remains untouched.

As they began their journey back home, the whispers guiding their every step, Timmy and Boxley knew that this was just the beginning of a grand adventure. Together, they would unlock the mysteries of the forest, discovering more about their own abilities with each step they took.

And so, hand in hand, Timmy and Boxley ventured forth, ready to face whatever challenges lay ahead, their hearts filled with hope and their minds filled with the secrets of the Whispering Winds.

Chapter 14: Unlocking Ancient Riddles

Timmy and Boxley stood in awe as they gazed upon the ancient tome lying open before them. Its weathered pages were inscribed with cryptic riddles that held the key to unlocking treasures hidden deep within the enchanted world they had come to love. Excitement coursed through their veins as they knew they were about to embark on their most challenging adventure yet.

With a determined look in their eyes, Timmy and Boxley began deciphering the first riddle. "In the land where fire meets ice, where the mountains reach the sky, lies a hidden gem stowed away. Seek it out, but beware the dragon's cry."

Puzzling over the riddle, Timmy and Boxley recalled their journeys through the enchanted world. They remembered a place where a mountain range was veiled in frost while fiery eruptions punctuated the surrounding landscape. It could only be the Dragon's Peak.

Without wasting a moment, Timmy and Boxley set off towards Dragon's Peak. As they trekked through thick forests and crossed treacherous rivers, they felt the anticipation building. Finally, they reached the mysterious mountain, its peak shrouded in mist.

As they climbed higher, the distant sound of a dragon's roar became more audible. Timmy's heart raced, but he knew they had to press on. They came upon a hidden cave at the mountain's summit and cautiously stepped inside.

In the dimly lit cave, Timmy and Boxley discovered a wall covered in ancient hieroglyphics. "Look, Boxley! These symbols might hold the key to solving the riddle," Timmy exclaimed.

Together, they studied the hieroglyphics, deciphering their meaning. The message revealed the secret of the hidden gem: "To obtain the gem, let golden light be your guide. In the reflection of fire, the path shall subside."

Curiosity sparked in their eyes as they understood the riddle's meaning. Golden light could only refer to sunlight, and the reflection of fire hinted at the dragon's flames. Timmy and Boxley realized they had to harness the power of the sun and redirect it through the fire's reflection to unlock the hidden gem.

They crafted intricate mirrors, expertly angled to capture the sun's rays and redirect them towards the golden flames. As the sunbeams met the flickering fire, a passage opened before their eyes, revealing a dazzling gem nestled within.

With cautious hands, Timmy reached out and retrieved the gem, marveling at its beauty. The room seemed to brighten as the gem emitted a radiant glow, tingling with ancient magic.

Timmy and Boxley had successfully solved the first riddle, but they knew their journey was far from over. With the gem in hand, they awaited a new challenge, wondering where the next riddle would lead them.

Little did they know, this was just the beginning of a treasure hunt that would test their intelligence, courage, and friendship. With each riddle solved, ancient secrets would unravel, leading them one step closer to unlocking the ultimate treasure hidden within the enchanted world.

Stay tuned for Chapter 15: The Mysterious Labyrinth, where Timmy and Boxley venture into a maze filled with illusion and mystery.

Chapter 15: A Magical Performance

Timmy and Boxley were thrilled at the thought of participating in the enchanted world's annual magical performance. They had been preparing for weeks, practicing their tricks and perfecting their act. With Boxley's natural sprite magic and Timmy's newfound skills, they were confident they could create something truly extraordinary.

On the day of the performance, Timmy and Boxley arrived at the grand theater, beaming with excitement. The theater was buzzing with magical beings from all corners of the enchanted world. Fairies, gnomes, unicorns, and even a dragon were there to witness the awe-inspiring talents of the performers.

As Timmy and Boxley waited backstage, they watched the incredible acts before them, mesmerized by the spells and illusions unfolding on the stage. The anticipation grew, and soon it was their turn to step into the limelight.

The stage lit up with colorful lights, and Boxley fluttered above in a shimmering glow. With a wave of his tiny hands, he conjured a group of dancing butterflies, twirling and fluttering gracefully in the air. The audience gasped in awe as Timmy joined in, his fingers emitting sparks that turned into sparklers, illuminating the butterflies' path.

Next, Timmy pulled a deck of enchanted cards from his pocket, their backs glowing with a mysterious aura. With a swift flick of his wrist, he commanded the cards to dance mid-air, forming breathtaking patterns and shapes. Boxley's magic lent them an extra flair, creating a kaleidoscope of colors that left the audience spellbound.

In their grand finale, Timmy and Boxley combined their powers. They created an illusion of a magical book floating in the air. As Timmy flipped the pages, the characters inside the book sprung to life, jumping and twirling in a mesmerizing dance.

The audience erupted into applause, their cheers echoing through the theater. Timmy and Boxley took their final bow, feeling a sense of accomplishment and pride. They knew they had delivered a performance that would be remembered for years to come.

Backstage, their friends, including Mia the fairy and Oliver the gnome, rushed to congratulate them. Mia's wings shimmered with excitement, and Oliver's beard curled with delight. They showered Timmy and Boxley with praises for their extraordinary act.

"You two were absolutely amazing!" Mia exclaimed, her voice filled with wonder. "I've never seen anything like it!"

Oliver nodded enthusiastically. "Indeed! Your tricks were out of this world. You truly are a magical duo!"

Timmy and Boxley exchanged satisfied glances, grateful for the support and encouragement from their friends. As they laughed and celebrated together, they couldn't help but feel a warm sense of camaraderie and a deep appreciation for the enchanting world they called home.

From that day forward, Timmy and Boxley became regular performers in the enchanted world's annual magical performance, wowing audiences year after year with their incredible acts. Together, they brought joy, wonder, and a touch of magic to the hearts of all who witnessed their extraordinary adventures on stage.

Chapter 16: The Parallel Worlds

Timmy's mind was buzzing with excitement as Boxley revealed the existence of parallel worlds. He had always wondered if there were different versions of himself and his sprite friend out there, living different adventures. Now, the thought of exploring these alternate universes filled him with an unparalleled sense of curiosity and wonder.

As they stood in the middle of the mystical forest, Timmy and Boxley prepared themselves for the incredible journey ahead. Boxley, being well-versed in the ways of the sprite world, explained that they needed to find a portal to travel between dimensions. Together, they set their sights on uncovering the gateway to these parallel worlds.

After a few hours of searching, their efforts paid off. They stumbled upon a hidden cave, shimmering with an otherworldly light. The entrance looked like an ordinary rabbit hole, but Boxley assured Timmy that it was indeed the portal they were looking for.

With a deep breath, Timmy took Boxley's hand, and together they jumped into the rabbit hole. The world around them instantly changed, and they found themselves in a parallel universe. The sky was a different hue, and the trees seemed to whisper unknown secrets.

Timmy and Boxley ventured forth, excited to meet alternate versions of themselves. It didn't take long before they stumbled upon a clearing, where a young Timmy was climbing a massive tree with a mischievous grin on his face. His sprite companion looked similar to Boxley but had a vibrant blue aura.

"Hello there!" Timmy called out, catching the attention of the parallel Timmy and his sprite. They both turned their heads, surprised to see someone addressing them.

Curiosity sparked in their eyes as they approached the duo. The parallel Timmy asked, "Who are you, and how do you know our names?"

Timmy and Boxley exchanged glances before explaining the concept of parallel worlds. The parallel Timmy was fascinated, while his sprite companion, Blakey, seemed skeptical at first. Soon, however, curiosity got the better of them, and they agreed to join forces.

As they continued exploring the parallel worlds, Timmy and Boxley encountered various versions of themselves, all leading extraordinary lives. In one world, Timmy had become a renowned scientist, and Boxley had transformed into a magnificent fire sprite, wielding great power. In another universe, they were explorers setting out on a grand quest.

Each encounter brought new insights and valuable experiences. The friends' bond grew stronger as they shared laughter, knowledge, and a sense of awe for the infinite possibilities within these parallel dimensions.

Yet, despite all the excitement, they felt a tug towards their home dimension. A longing for their own adventures, their original world where their families awaited. Acknowledging this, they turned towards the portal that would take them back.

Timmy and Boxley bid farewell to their parallel counterparts, knowing they had made lifelong connections and memories. With a final step through the rabbit hole, they returned to their beloved forest.

As they emerged from the hidden cave, Timmy and Boxley smiled at each other. The parallel worlds had given them incredible adventures and invaluable knowledge. Though their heads were filled with the wonders of what lay beyond, they were content to be home. They were excited to continue their own adventures, together, with new perspectives and the memories of those they had met.

And so, with eyes twinkling and hearts brimming with new stories, Timmy and Boxley set off on their next thrilling adventure, eager to see how their experiences in the parallel worlds would shape their futures.

Chapter 17: Facing the Shadow Beast

Timmy and Boxley stood at the entrance of a dark, eerie cave, their hearts pounding with fear. Inside, a deep growl echoed through the walls, as if taunting them to come closer. The air grew colder, and their surroundings became shrouded in darkness. This was the lair of the dreaded Shadow Beast.

Timmy's hands trembled, but he knew he had to face his greatest fear head-on. Beside him, Boxley, his loyal sprite friend, emitted a faint glow, providing a reassuring light in the darkness. "Don't worry, Timmy. We'll get through this together," Boxley said, his voice filled with determination.

Taking a deep breath, Timmy stepped forward, clutching onto Boxley tightly. As they ventured deeper into the cave, the growling grew louder, sending shivers down their spines. Suddenly, the Shadow Beast emerged from the shadows, its form shifting and writhing, taking the shape of their darkest fears.

Timmy's heart raced as the Shadow Beast transformed into a giant spider, its glaring eyes fixed on him. His fear of spiders rushed back, paralyzing him with terror. Boxley gently nudged him, reminding him of their courage. "Timmy, remember, you're stronger than any fear. You have the power to face it and overcome it!"

Summoning every ounce of his willpower, Timmy pushed through the paralyzing fear, reminding himself that this was just an illusion, a test of his inner strength. He closed his eyes, visualizing a bright light surrounding him, making him feel safe and protected.

With a newfound sense of bravery, Timmy opened his eyes, facing the Shadow Beast head-on. He reached deep within himself, finding a well of courage he didn't know he possessed. As he stared directly into the Beast's eyes, he realized that the beast was merely a reflection of his own insecurities, doubts, and fears.

"I am not afraid," Timmy shouted, his voice filled with conviction. "You are just a manifestation of my own shadow. I am stronger than you!"

As Timmy spoke these words, the Shadow Beast began to shrink and weaken, its power diminishing with each passing moment. It thrashed and roared in frustration, but its presence grew fainter and fainter.

Finally, the Shadow Beast vanished completely, leaving only a sense of triumph and self-belief in its wake. Timmy and Boxley stood side by side, their hearts filled with pride and newfound strength. They had conquered their fears and emerged victorious.

As they exited the cave, Timmy and Boxley looked at each other, their bond deeper than ever. They had not only faced the Shadow Beast but had also learned a valuable lesson about the power of facing their own shadows. From that day forward, they vowed to confront their fears head-on and to never let their shadows hold them back.

And so, with their heads held high and hearts brimming with courage, Timmy and Boxley continued on their adventures, ready to face whatever challenges lay ahead, knowing that they had the strength to overcome anything as long as they believed in themselves.

Chapter 18: The Reunion of Friends

As Timmy and Boxley journeyed through the enchanted forest, they could hardly contain their excitement. It had been a while since they had seen their enchanted friends from their previous adventures, and the prospect of being reunited filled their hearts with joy.

The two friends arrived at a clearing in the forest, where all their friends were waiting for them. There was Sparkle, the mischievous fairy, with her bright blue wings shimmering in the sunlight. Hopper, the wise old owl, perched on a branch above, his golden eyes sparkling with wisdom. And there, standing proud and regal, was Gracie, the unicorn, her coat glistening in shades of silver and gold.

As Timmy and Boxley approached, their friends erupted in cheers and applause. They embraced Timmy and Boxley tightly, sharing in the warmth of their reunion. It was a moment of pure happiness, a reminder of the bond they all shared.

They settled down in the clearing, the rustling leaves providing a soothing backdrop to their conversations. Each of their friends took turns sharing the adventures they had encountered while Timmy and Boxley were away.

Sparkle recounted how she had traveled to the Land of Fireflies, a magical realm where every night was like a breathtaking light show. She spoke of making new fairy friends and learning enchanting spells that would make the stars dance in the sky.

Hopper spoke of his pilgrimage to the Hidden Library, a secret place known only to the wise beings of the forest. There, he discovered ancient books and scrolls that contained knowledge beyond his wildest dreams. He had spent countless nights deep in study, unlocking even more of the forest's secrets.

And Gracie, with a hint of nostalgia in her eyes, shared her journey through the Whispering Woods. She had encountered a tribe of gentle forest creatures who spoke in hushed tones and shared stories of love and friendship. It was there that Gracie had learned the true power of unity and the importance of fighting for what is right.

As each story unfolded, Timmy and Boxley marveled at the incredible journeys their friends had undertaken. They realized that their separate adventures had resulted in personal growth and a newfound appreciation for the power of friendship.

"This reunion has made me realize how much we mean to one another," Timmy said, an earnest smile lighting up his face. "No matter where we go or what we face, our bond is unbreakable."

Boxley nodded in agreement, feeling a deep sense of gratitude for his friends. "It's true," he said. "We impact each other's lives in ways we may never fully comprehend. Our adventures make us stronger, but it's our friendship that truly brings us joy."

The friends spent the rest of the day celebrating their reunion, sharing laughter, and creating new memories. They danced beneath the moonlight, shared stories around a crackling fire, and promised to never let their adventures separate them again.

In the enchanted forest, Timmy and Boxley had discovered a priceless gift – the gift of friendship. And as they continued their journey, they knew that no matter where life took them, their friends would forever hold a special place in their hearts.

Chapter 19: The Grand Finale

It was a beautiful morning in the magical land of Pixtopia, as the sun rose on the horizon, casting a golden glow over the majestic landscape. Timmy and Boxley stood together, ready to embark on their most extraordinary adventure yet.

Their friends from all the magical realms had gathered to help them in their final quest. There was Lily, the water nymph, with her calming presence and ability to manipulate water at will. Next to her was Blaze, the fiery dragon, who possessed an incredible power to harness the element of fire. On the other side stood Zephyr, the mischievous gnome, who could control the wind and bring forth gusts of wind when needed.

Timmy and Boxley had grown closer to all their friends over the course of their previous adventures, and together they formed an unstoppable team, ready to face any challenge that awaited them. They were determined to protect the magical realms from any darkness that threatened to consume them.

As their journey began, they retraced their steps through the enchanted forest, casting spells and solving puzzles they had encountered before. The friends encountered mystical creatures they had met along their previous adventures, who offered their assistance and guidance.

With each challenge they faced, Timmy and Boxley grew stronger and more confident. They fought off the wicked forest sprites by using Lily's water magic. They overcame treacherous lava pits with Blaze's fire-breathing abilities. And they soared through the air with Zephyr's gusts of wind, evading the airborne creatures that guarded their path.

Through it all, Timmy's determination and Boxley's cunning strategies led them closer to their ultimate goal – to save the realms from the impending darkness. Along their journey, they discovered hidden treasures and ancient artifacts that gave them strength and power.

Finally, after days of trekking through enchanted lands and battling powerful adversaries, they reached the heart of the mystical realms. There, they encountered the dark sorcerer, Malachi, who had been orchestrating all the chaos that threatened the realms.

With all their might and the help of their friends, Timmy and Boxley faced Malachi head-on. He unleashed his dark magic, but they countered with their combined powers. Lily held back his dark spells with her water magic, while Blaze engulfed him in his fiery wrath. Zephyr summoned a powerful gust of wind, disorienting Malachi and giving Timmy and Boxley the chance to strike.

The battle intensified, as the friends fought valiantly. Timmy and Boxley did not falter and poured their hearts into every move they made. They knew that the fate of Pixtopia and all the magical realms rested on their shoulders.

In a final act of bravery, Timmy and Boxley unleashed their most powerful attack, their combined forces colliding with Malachi's dark magic. The entire realm shook, as a blinding light enveloped the battlefield.

When the light faded, Timmy and Boxley stood victorious. The darkness that had once threatened the realms had been vanquished, and peace was restored.

With tears of joy and relief, Timmy and Boxley were hailed as heroes by the grateful inhabitants of Pixtopia. They were honored and celebrated for their courage and determination.

As their adventures came to an end, Timmy and Boxley knew that they would forever cherish the memories they had created and the friends they had made along the way. Their extraordinary journey had taught them the value of friendship, bravery, and the power of believing in oneself.

And so, as the sun set over the magical land of Pixtopia, Timmy and Boxley bid farewell to their friends, knowing that their incredible adventure had left an indelible mark on their hearts. They walked off into the sunset, ready for new adventures, and with the knowledge that they could overcome any challenge that came their way.

Chapter 20: A Farewell and a Promise

Timmy and Boxley stood at the edge of the magical forest, taking in the sight of their friends bidding them farewell. The forest was alive with vibrant colors, as if nature itself was celebrating their achievements. The fairies fluttered around, sprinkling sparkles of magic in the air, while the talking animals chattered happily, their voices filled with gratitude.

King Oberon stepped forward, his regal demeanor shining through. "Timmy, Boxley, you have brought light and joy to our realm," he said solemnly. "You are forever part of our magical tapestry, and the memories of our adventures will live on in your hearts."

Timmy felt a lump forming in his throat. He never wanted this journey to end, but he had to return to his own world. Boxley, sensing his friend's sadness, nudged him gently, a comforting smile on his face.

Queen Titania floated gracefully to Timmy's side, her voice soft and soothing. "Dear

Timmy, we have watched you grow throughout this journey. You have shown courage, kindness, and a deep love for the magic that exists in our world. Carry these qualities with you always, and may they guide you in your own realm."

Timmy wiped away a few stray tears, his voice catching. "I will always remember the magic of this place and the friends I have made. Whenever I feel sad or alone, I will think of you all, and the memories will lift my spirits."

The fairies gathered around, embracing Timmy and Boxley in a flurry of tiny wings. They whispered their own goodbyes, their enchanting voices wrapping around the boys like a warm hug. The talking animals trotted up, nudging their legs affectionately, communicating their gratitude without words.

As the farewells continued, Timmy noticed a familiar face emerging from the crowd. It was Willow, the wise and kindhearted tree spirit they had encountered many adventures ago. Her branches rustled gently, and she spoke with a voice that echoed through the forest.

"Timmy, my dear child, remember that magic is not limited to one place. Carry the spirit of adventure and wonder with you always. Seek joy in the simplest of things, and remember that the bonds you have formed here will never truly fade."

Timmy nodded, feeling a renewed strength building within him. He knew that even though he was leaving, he would never truly be apart from his friends. They were forever connected through the magic they had shared, and their bond would span across worlds.

After the farewells were complete, Timmy and Boxley returned home. The magical forest faded away, leaving them standing on the familiar path that led to their neighborhood. The memories of their adventures still burned brightly in their minds, and they knew they had been forever changed.

As they walked through their front door, Timmy turned to Boxley with a smile. "We may be home now, but the magic will always be with us. We'll never forget our incredible journey or the friends we made along the way. And who knows, Boxley? Perhaps one day the magic will bring us all together again."

Boxley nodded, a mischievous glimmer in his eyes. "Indeed, Timmy. The magic has a way of weaving destinies together. Our adventure may have come to an end, but a new one always lies just around the corner."

And so, Timmy and Boxley settled back into their normal lives, forever cherishing the remarkable bond they had formed and the memories of their amazing adventures. They knew that even in the mundane, they would find traces of magic, always reminding them that the extraordinary can exist in the most unexpected places.

Chapter 21: The Mysterious Map

Timmy and Boxley had spent countless hours exploring the attic, but today they stumbled upon something truly extraordinary. Buried amidst dusty old books and forgotten treasures, they uncovered a worn piece of parchment—an ancient map.

Intrigued by its peculiar markings, the duo carefully unfurled the delicate paper. The map depicted a sprawling landscape with mountains, rivers, and secret pathways. But what caught Timmy's attention the most were the mysterious symbols etched along the edges.

"What do you think these markings mean, Boxley?" Timmy pondered, his eyes jumping from one symbol to another.

Boxley, the sprightly sprite with abundant knowledge about enchanted artifacts, floated closer to get a better look. "These markings, Timmy, appear to be some sort of ancient code," he observed. "It seems that they hold the key to unraveling the secrets of this map."

Timmy's eyes widened with excitement. "We have to decipher it, Boxley! Imagine the adventures and treasures that await us if we can unlock its hidden secrets."

Determined to crack the code, Timmy and Boxley scurried downstairs to gather their wits and some useful tools. They rummaged through their collection of books, searching for any information that could help them decipher the map's enigmatic symbols.

After hours of dedicated research, Timmy and Boxley discovered an old tome entitled "The Lost Legends and Cryptic Codes: A Guide to Ancient Treasures." Gingerly turning its brittle pages, they came across a chapter that discussed similar symbols to those on the map.

The book explained that each symbol represented a specific element of nature, such as fire, water, earth, or air. It also revealed that combining these elements in a certain order could unveil the map's hidden message.

Without wasting a moment, Timmy and Boxley carefully traced the symbols on the map and arranged them in accordance with their newfound knowledge. As each symbol aligned perfectly, a glorious glow emanated from the parchment, transforming it into a three-dimensional holographic projection of the mystery landscape.

Timmy and Boxley were awe-struck as they stood in the midst of the shimmering projection. It seemed as if the map had sprung to life, offering them an invitation to embark on a grand adventure.

Following the guidance of the map, our heroes set out on their quest to locate the legendary Horn of Eldoria—a powerful artifact known to grant its possessor the power to communicate with mystical creatures.

The map guided them through treacherous terrains filled with towering cliffs, ancient ruins, and dense forests teeming with mythical beasts. Timmy and Boxley faced numerous challenges and overcame them with bravery and resourcefulness, relying on their friendship and unwavering determination.

Finally, after weeks of trials and tribulations, Timmy and Boxley found themselves standing before a towering waterfall. Faithfully following the map's instructions, they touched a hidden glyph on a nearby boulder, causing the waterfall to part, revealing a hidden cave behind it.

Heart pounding with excitement, they ventured into the depths of the cave, where they discovered a glimmering chamber containing the fabled Horn of Eldoria.

As they held the artifact in their hands, they felt an indescribable surge of power and a connection to the magical realms. Little did they know that their journey had only just begun, setting the stage for even greater adventures alongside the mystical beings who awaited their call.

With the map leading the way, Timmy, Boxley, and the Horn of Eldoria commenced a new chapter in their extraordinary adventures, brimming with enchanted friendships, unexpected perils, and unforgettable quests in the realms beyond imagination.

Chapter 22: The Enchanted Forest

As Timmy and Boxley followed the map's directions, the dense trees of the ordinary forest transformed into an extraordinary sight. The once familiar chirping of birds and rustling leaves now hummed with a melodious tune. The air was filled with a sweet scent, as if the winds were carrying the aroma of blooming flowers from afar.

With wide-eyed astonishment, Timmy and Boxley stepped into the Enchanted Forest. The trees stood tall, their trunks adorned with vibrant moss that glowed in various hues. The sunlight peeked through the canopy above, casting beautiful patterns on the forest floor.

"You ready for this, Boxley?" Timmy asked, excitement evident in his voice.

"Absolutely, Timmy! This forest is full of wonders, and I can't wait to explore them all," replied Boxley, fluttering alongside his friend.

As they cautiously moved forward, the ground beneath them began to change. Suddenly, the grass turned into squishy moss, bouncing back with every step they took. Timmy and Boxley giggled, bouncing around like kangaroos until they reached a massive rainbow waterfall.

Timmy and Boxley stared awestruck as the water cascaded down, creating a vivid rainbow arch. They soon spotted a wooden bridge leading to the other side, but it seemed rickety and unpredictable.

"How will we cross it, Timmy?" asked Boxley, trying to figure out a way.

Timmy, putting his problem-solving skills to the test, replied, "We'll have to be careful with each step, Boxley. Let's hold hands and take it slow."

With a deep breath, they took their first step, feeling the bridge sway beneath them. Timmy kept his eyes focused, his determination overriding any fear. Boxley, a small guardian spirit, used his light to guide their way, illuminating the path ahead.

After what seemed like an eternity, they reached the other side of the bridge. Relieved, they high-fived each other, proud of their accomplishment.

Their journey through the Enchanted Forest continued, uncovering many more marvels. They encountered talking animals who shared stories of their adventures, mysterious fairies who sprinkled magical dust, and towering mushrooms they could climb on.

In the midst of their exploration, they stumbled upon a hidden trail leading to a cleared area guarded by stone statues. Curiosity getting the better of them, they decided to investigate.

As they ventured into the clearing, a deep voice echoed, "Who dares enter the sacred forest of the Ancients?"

Timmy and Boxley looked around, trying to locate the source of the voice. Suddenly, the stone statues sprung to life, their eyes glowing a fiery red.

With courage bolstered by their previous triumphs, Timmy stepped forward and replied, "I am Timmy, and this is Boxley, a brave sprite. We mean no harm and only seek the wonders this forest holds."

The statues looked at each other, seemingly assessing Timmy's sincerity. After a moment, their fiery glow dimmed, and they returned to their inactive state. The voice reassured, "You have proven your intentions. Explore the forest and learn its secrets, young ones."

Grateful for their safe passage, Timmy and Boxley continued their enchanting journey, eager to unravel the remaining mysteries of the Enchanted Forest.

Little did they know, their bravery and problem-solving skills were preparing them for the ultimate challenge that awaited them at the heart of the forest.

Chapter 23: The Guardian of the Treasure

Timmy and Boxley stood at the entrance of a magnificent clearing in the heart of the Enchanted Forest. It was said that within this hidden haven lay the fabled Treasure of the Ancients. The foliage around them whispered with excitement as the duo prepared themselves to confront the Guardian, the powerful creature charged with protecting the riches within.

As they stepped forward, the gentle rustling of leaves intensified, and a shimmering figure materialized before them. The Guardian of the Treasure stood tall and imposing, its body adorned with intricate patterns that seemed to dance with every move.

"Who dares approach the Treasure? Speak now, for only those who prove their worthiness shall be allowed passage," boomed the Guardian's voice, resonating through the forest.

Timmy took a deep breath, his heart pounding with a mixture of fear and determination. He looked at Boxley, who gave an encouraging nod, their eyes reflecting the same unwavering determination.

"We are Timmy and Boxley," Timmy began, his voice steady. "We have journeyed through perilous lands, overcoming trials and tribulations to reach this point. Our hearts are pure, and our intentions are noble. We seek the Treasure not for personal gain but to restore balance and bring peace to our world."

Boxley floated beside Timmy, adding, "We understand the magnitude of this responsibility, Guardian. We honor the ancient ways and promise to protect and cherish the Treasure while using its power for the greater good."

The Guardian's eyes stared deep into their souls, as if examining their very essence. It seemed to sense the sincerity in their words, yet it remained unmoving. Suddenly, the forest fell silent, and the air became thick with anticipation.

To demonstrate their worthiness, Timmy and Boxley knew they needed to prove their mettle. They exchanged determined glances before Timmy stepped forward, holding out his hand. From within his palm, a tiny sapling emerged, slowly growing into a majestic oak tree.

"Guardian, witness the power of life and growth," Timmy declared, his voice commanding yet gentle. "We stand before you as guardians of the natural world, with the ability to nurture and protect."

As the oak tree reached its full glory, flowers blossomed, and birds nestled within its branches. The Guardian watched in silent awe, finally acknowledging the duo's connection to the spirit world.

Impressed, the Guardian slowly lowered its mighty arm and spoke, its voice filled with wisdom. "You have proven yourselves worthy of the Treasure, young defenders. May its power be bestowed upon you, for your intentions are noble and your hearts are pure."

With those words, a brilliant stream of light enveloped Timmy and Boxley, encasing them in a protective aura. The Guardian, satisfied with their worthiness, then stepped aside, revealing a hidden pathway leading to the coveted Treasure.

Timmy and Boxley exchanged a triumphant smile before stepping forward, their hearts full of gratitude. They moved ahead, confident that they had gained the trust of the Guardian and were now one step closer to their ultimate goal.

Little did they know; the challenge with the Guardian was nothing compared to the trials awaiting them within the depths of the

Treasury. But with their newfound connection to the spirit world, they were ready to face any obstacle that lay ahead.

Together, Timmy and Boxley ventured deeper into the enchanted forest, their spirits soaring high, for they knew that beyond the Treasure's wealth awaited a destiny far greater than they could ever fathom.

Chapter 24: The Hidden Vault

Timmy's heart raced in anticipation as he and Boxley stood before the ancient doors of the hidden vault. With trembling hands, Timmy took out the map and whispered the final clue to himself, trying to decipher its meaning.

"The path is clear, the treasure near, but danger lurks beyond the light. Together we must stay, for only in unity can we fight."

Timmy glanced at Boxley, who nodded with determination. They both knew the risks they were about to face, but their determination to uncover the secrets of the hidden vault outweighed their fear.

As the doors creaked open, Timmy and Boxley stepped into an ethereal chamber bathed in a golden glow. Their eyes widened in awe at the sight before them. The vault was filled with shelves adorned with glistening jewels, shimmering artifacts, and ancient scrolls.

Entranced by the mesmerizing display, they slowly made their way deeper into the vault, their footsteps echoing through the chamber. The exhilaration of their surroundings momentarily pushed the looming danger to the back of their minds.

But suddenly, the shadows in the corners of the room seemed to grow darker and more menacing. A feeling of unease crept over Timmy, causing him to shiver involuntarily. Boxley, ever watchful, sensed it too.

Just as they exchanged worried glances, a low growl reverberated through the chamber, sending a chill down their spines. The air grew heavy, and the room seemed to close in around them.

Timmy and Boxley glanced around, their hazel eyes darting from one shadowy corner to another. They knew they were not alone.

Dread filled their hearts, but they steeled themselves, clinging onto the hope that their unity would carry them through.

Suddenly, two glowing eyes shone in the darkness, followed by a sinister laugh that echoed through the vault. The danger had revealed itself – a menacing figure draped in a cloak of darkness, its true form concealed.

With a wave of its hand, the shadows danced and twisted, forming wicked claws that glinted menacingly in the dim light. Timmy and Boxley stood back to back, their bond stronger than ever as they prepared to face the lurking danger.

As the figure lunged towards them, Timmy and Boxley fought valiantly, their courage fueling their every move. The sprite darted through the air, leaving trails of sparkling light in its wake, while Timmy swung his trusty wooden sword with all his might.

The clash of steel against darkness, the shimmers and flashes of light against the undulating shadows, marked the beginning of an epic battle. Timmy and Boxley fought with unwavering determination, their eyes locked on each other, communicating silently in their shared effort to combat the lurking danger.

For what felt like hours, they dodged each strike, countered every move, and slowly inched closer to their foe. The vault reverberated with the fierce energy of the battle, as if the echoes of their determination resonated through time itself.

Finally, with one final strike, Timmy's sword pierced through the figure's cloak, dispersing the darkness into thin air. The chamber fell silent, the tension dissipating like smoke, as they stood triumphant over the vanquished danger.

Exhausted but filled with a sense of accomplishment, Timmy and Boxley caught their breath. They had overcome the lurking danger within the hidden vault, closer than ever to uncovering its secrets.

Little did they know that even greater trials and astonishing discoveries awaited them as they continued their adventures in the hidden vault.

Chapter 25: Trapped!

As Timmy and Boxley ventured deeper into the enchanted forest, they came across a peculiar clearing. The air was filled with an eerie stillness, and the long shadows stretched ominously across the ground. Sensing danger, Boxley urged Timmy to be cautious, but curiosity got the better of them, and they approached the clearing with trepidation.

Little did they know, a cunning trapster had been lying in wait. With a mischievous smirk, he activated a hidden mechanism, causing the ground beneath Timmy and Boxley to crumble away. Before they could react, they found themselves falling into a dark pit.

As they landed with a thud, Timmy and Boxley quickly realized they were trapped inside a vault. The trapster had thought of everything – the walls were made of solid steel, and there were no visible exits.

Feeling trapped, Timmy was about to panic when Boxley reminded him of their resourcefulness. "Don't worry, Timmy," Boxley said with determination. "Remember all the challenges we've overcome before? We'll find a way out of here too!"

Looking around, Timmy noticed a small, flickering light coming from a crack in the wall. Curiosity piqued, he approached it and discovered a tiny key lying on the ground. Excited, Timmy picked it up and showed it to Boxley.

"I bet this is the key to our escape!" Timmy exclaimed. They tried it on the vault door, but to their dismay, it didn't fit. Undeterred, they decided to explore the vault in search of additional clues.

As they ventured deeper into the vault, they found cryptic writings etched on the walls. Boxley, being a sprite with immense knowledge, deciphered the ancient script. The writings revealed that the key they had found was a part of a puzzle – a puzzle that would unveil the true exit.

With newfound determination, Timmy and Boxley closely examined the writings and discovered a series of symbols and riddles. Their challenge was to solve each riddle, decipher each symbol, and find the corresponding key hidden within the vault.

The first riddle stumped them for a moment, but their clever minds eventually uncovered the solution. They found the corresponding key hidden beneath a loose floorboard. Excitedly, they hurried back to the vault door and tried the key once again. This time, it clicked into place, and the door swung open, revealing a dimly lit corridor beyond.

As Timmy and Boxley cautiously stepped into the corridor, they realized their adventure was far from over. With their wits and resourcefulness, they were determined to escape their captor's clutches and continue their quest to save the enchanted forest.

Little did they know, danger lurked around every corner, and the cunning trapster was hot on their trail. But with the bond of friendship between Timmy and Boxley stronger than ever, they were ready to face any challenge that awaited them.

Chapter 26: Unlikely Allies

Timmy and Boxley had been stuck in the underground vault for what felt like an eternity. They were growing tired and desperate, because no matter how hard they tried, they couldn't find a way to escape. Their hopes were dwindling, until one fateful day, they stumbled upon a hidden chamber tucked away behind an old bookshelf.

As they cautiously entered the chamber, they discovered a peculiar sight. A group of misfit creatures, ranging in shapes and sizes, were gathered together, huddled in a circle. There was an impish goblin, a winged pixie, a crafty gnome, and even a wise old dragon, among others. Timmy and Boxley couldn't believe their eyes – they had found a group of unlikely allies!

With curiosity and excitement, Timmy and Boxley approached the group. The creatures looked up, startled, as their eyes met. Timmy, eager to explain their situation, quickly shared their story – how they ended up in the vault and their desperate need for a plan to escape.

The misfit creatures listened attentively. The goblin, known as Grumchuck, had an ear-to-ear grin on his face. "Well, well, well, looks like we've got ourselves some brave adventurers here!" he exclaimed. "We might just have the perfect plan to outsmart that dastardly trapster!"

The pixie, named Twinklewings, chimed in with her high-pitched voice. "Indeed, we each have our own unique talents that can help us overcome any obstacle!" she said. "I can use my magical powers to create illusions and distractions."

The gnome, named Tinkerfoot, nodded in agreement. "And I have an innate ability to unlock and disarm mechanical traps," he said with a mischievous glint in his eye. "We'll need that to trick the trapster and escape his clutches."

The group continued to exchange their skills and talents. Boxley, being a sprite, possessed incredible speed and agility, which would come in handy during their escape. The old dragon, called Emberheart, had a vast knowledge of the trapster's hideouts and the secrets of the surrounding dungeons.

With every passing minute, their plan grew more precisely. Timmy and Boxley were amazed at the creativity and resourcefulness of their new allies. It seemed that fate had brought them together, each possessing something unique and crucial to their escape.

Days turned into weeks as they meticulously devised their plan. They studied the vault's layout, dismantled traps, and created diversion tactics. Through their collaboration, trust between the group of misfits and Timmy and Boxley grew stronger each day. They were no longer just companions; they were a team, united by their common goal.

Finally, the day of the great escape arrived. With their plan in motion, they set out to outsmart the trapster and regain their freedom. Timmy, Boxley, Grumchuck, Twinklewings, Tinkerfoot, and Emberheart moved as one, skillfully executing the plan they had molded over countless nights.

The trapster had no idea what hit him. The combined efforts of their diverse skills and knowledge left him bewildered and caught off guard. Every trap he had so carefully designed and set up was swiftly avoided or disarmed, much to his frustration.

With their freedom just within reach, the group made their way towards the vault's exit. They could practically taste the sweet air of liberation awaiting them. But as they approached the final hurdle, they knew their greatest challenge still lay ahead.

As they prepared to face the trapster for the last time, they huddled together, ready to give it their all. They had become more than just allies; they were a family. And with their newfound unity and determination, they were certain that no obstacle could stand in their way.

Chapter 27: The Battle for Freedom

Timmy and Boxley had finally found the secret vault where the missing treasures of Pixie Hollow were hidden. But little did they know that the notorious trapster had discovered their location. The trapster, a cunning villain with a knack for designing deadly traps, was determined to keep Timmy, Boxley, and their newfound allies trapped inside the vault forever.

As the group ventured deeper into the vault, a loud creak followed by a thunderous crash echoed through the stone corridors. The trapster's attack had begun. Timmy, Boxley, and their friends found themselves surrounded by an army of mechanical spiders, their sharp metal limbs clawing at the air.

"Boxley, we need a plan!" Timmy exclaimed, his voice trembling with both fear and determination.

Boxley, being a sprite well-versed in strategy, quickly assessed the situation. "We can't fight those spiders head-on. We need to outsmart them," he said, his eyes darting around the room for any possible advantages.

Spotting a control panel on the wall, Boxley's eyes sparkled with mischief. "I have an idea, but you'll have to trust me," he said, turning to Timmy.

Timmy nodded, his trust in his sprite friend unwavering. "Lead the way, Boxley."

Working swiftly, Boxley dashed towards the control panel while Timmy and their friends engaged in a fierce battle with the mechanical spiders. With each swing of their weapons and dodge of the spiders' attacks, they fought valiantly. But the enemy seemed relentless, their numbers seemingly multiplying by the minute.

Finally, Boxley reached the control panel. With a mischievous grin, he pulled a lever marked "Emergency Override" and pressed a sequence of buttons. Suddenly, the stone ceiling began to shift, revealing hidden trapdoors in the floor. The mechanical spiders, confused by the sudden change in their environment, stumbled and fell into the traps.

With the spiders disposed of, Timmy and his friends cautiously made their way forward. But the trapster wasn't going to give up so easily. As they progressed, they encountered wall-sized blades swinging precariously from side to side and floors that disappeared beneath their feet, revealing treacherous spikes.

In this dire situation, Timmy and Boxley's teamwork and resourcefulness shone forth. Boxley used his intuition and nimbleness to deactivate the traps, while Timmy relied on his strength and quick reflexes to protect their friends from harm's way. Together, they dodged blades and leaped over pitfalls, inching closer to freedom with every passing second.

As they reached the final chamber, they found themselves facing the trapster himself, a wicked grin spread across his face. "You may have made it this far, but you won't escape me!" he sneered.

But Timmy, driven by his unwavering determination, charged forward alongside his friends. The battle that ensued was like no other they had encountered. Timmy used his brawn to overpower the trapster, while Boxley used his wit and agility to outmaneuver him.

Sparks flew as metal clashed against metal, and the room echoed with grunts and growls. But in the end, Timmy and Boxley's relentless spirit and unity triumphed. With a final maneuver, they managed to immobilize the trapster, leaving him defeated and at their mercy.

Gasping for breath, Timmy and Boxley stood victorious, surrounded by their weary but elated allies. The battle for freedom had been won, and the treasures of Pixie Hollow were finally reclaimed. The vault's doors swung open, revealing a world of beauty and wonder beyond their wildest dreams.

As they stepped out into the sunlight, Timmy couldn't help but feel a surge of pride and gratitude towards his friends. With their unwavering support and unwavering spirit, they had overcome all odds and emerged victoriously. And now, their adventures could continue, knowing that no obstacle was too great for them to conquer together.

Little did they know, even greater challenges awaited them in the magical realm of Pixie Hollow. But armed with bravery, friendship, and the lessons they learned in their battles, Timmy and Boxley were ready to face whatever came their way, side by side.

Chapter 28: The Return Home

With the treasure securely tucked away in their backpacks, Timmy and Boxley took one last look at the magical forest that had become their home, their hearts filled with gratitude for the incredible adventure they had just experienced. The sun's golden rays filtered through the leaves, creating a mesmerizing kaleidoscope of colors that danced around them.

"Boxley, I can't believe we're leaving this enchanting place," Timmy said, his voice laced with a hint of sadness.

"I know, Timmy," Boxley replied, his voice tinged with nostalgia. "But remember, we'll always have the memories and the friendships we made here."

Timmy nodded, his eyes misty with tears. Although excited to return home, he would miss the magical creatures and the forest's beauty. But as he looked down at Boxley, his loyal sprite friend, a smile began to creep across his face. They had each other, and their bond would last far beyond their time in the forest.

With one final wave to the forest creatures who had become their friends, Timmy and

Boxley turned towards the path that would lead them home. As they walked, their steps were lighter, and their hearts filled with anticipation for the stories they would tell and the plans they would make for future adventures.

As they approached the edge of the forest, the familiar sights and sounds of their town filled their senses. The bustling streets, the laughter of children playing, and the comforting smell of home greeted them warmly. It was as if they had never left.

Timmy's parents had been worried sick during their days away, but relief washed over their faces as they spotted Timmy and Boxley walking hand in hand towards them.

"Timmy!" his mother exclaimed, rushing forward to envelop him in a tight embrace.

"We were so worried," his father added, his voice filled with a mix of relief and sternness.

Timmy smiled up at them, sensing their love and concern. "I'm sorry, Mom and Dad, but you won't believe the incredible adventure we had!" he exclaimed, pulling out the treasure from his backpack and sharing the amazing story of their time in the magical forest.

As Timmy recounted their encounters with talking animals, flying dragons, and mischievous fairies, his parents' eyes widened in wonder. They listened intently to every word, captivated by the vividness of his storytelling.

After hearing the entire tale, Timmy's parents exchanged amazed glances. They couldn't believe the incredible journey their son had been on, but the sparkle in his eyes and the joy radiating from his face assured them it was all true.

Boxley, too, shared in their excitement, eagerly chiming in whenever Timmy forgot a detail or needed a nudge in remembering something important. As Timmy's mom and dad listened, they couldn't help but feel grateful for the magical sprite's presence in their son's life.

From that day forward, Timmy and Boxley were inseparable. They spent hours planning their next adventure, sketching maps, and discussing mythical creatures. Timmy's parents marveled at the strength of their friendship and encouraged their thirst for knowledge and exploration.

As Timmy and Boxley sat under the shade of their favorite oak tree, dreaming about the endless possibilities that awaited them, they knew their incredible adventure had only just begun. With their imaginations ignited, Timmy and Boxley vowed to continue exploring the wonders of the world together, their bond and love for adventure stronger than ever.

And so, their tale continues, with Timmy and Boxley ready to embark on countless more adventures, one magical chapter at a time.

Printed in Great Britain
by Amazon